THE VALENTINE'S DAY CARD

Amish Romance

HANNAH MILLER

Tica House
Publishing
Sweet Romance that Delights and Enchants!

Personal Word from the Author

To My Dear Readers,

How exciting that you have chosen one of my books to read. Thank you! I am proud to now be part of the team of writers at Tica House Publishing who work joyfully to bring you stories of hope, faith, courage, and love.

Please feel free to contact me as I love to hear from my readers. I would like to personally invite you to sign up for updates and to become part of our **Exclusive Reader Club** —it's completely Free to join! Hope to see you there!

With love,

Hannah Miller

VISIT HERE to Join our Reader's Club and to Receive Tica House Updates:

https://amish.subscribemenow.com/

Chapter One

Collette Bontrager peered out the frost-covered the window. It was hard to see much of anything through the darkness, but she strained her eyes hoping for a glimpse of Ivan Yordy's buggy coming up the drive. Yet nothing was moving outside except the top of the trees rippling in the wind.

She sighed and turned away from the window, her shoulders drooping. He'd said he'd be there by six, and it was after seven now. It wasn't like Ivan to be late when he'd promised to come to pick her up so they could go out for supper together. They'd been courting for over three years now, and he'd always been on time before. Had there been an accident? Was he ill?

Collette fretted silently. Something dreadful must have happened to cause Ivan's tardiness. She didn't know what to do. She couldn't ask her father to go to Ivan's and check on him. For some reason, her father wasn't a huge fan of Ivan's. She had no idea why he disliked him so, but she knew asking him to make the long ride to the Yordys' this evening wasn't a good plan.

Maybe if she went to her cousins' house, she could talk Jesse into going. She was often going over to visit with Esther, so it shouldn't raise any suspicions with her parents. It was cold, yes, but the night was clear, and the roads were in fairly good shape. Maybe Jesse would do it for her.

"*Daed*, do you think I could go spend the night with Esther?" Collette turned pleading blue eyes on her father. "I would like to help her with the *boppli* clothes she's making for her sister."

Abner raised his eyebrows and looked at Collette. "What about your plans with Ivan, *dochder*?"

Colette flushed and looked down at her shoes. How she wished her parents still didn't know about her courtship with Ivan. But they'd found out, and now they talked about it freely. "Um, something must have come up. If he does show up, *Mamm* or you can send him to Esther's."

Abner rubbed his beard thoughtfully for a moment and Collette held her breath while he considered her request. "Well, I s'pose spending the night with your cousins ain't such a bad idea. I guess I could take you there."

"*Denki, Daed*. I'll just grab a few things and we can go when you're ready." Collette was practically trembling with relief. She could not put down her worry that something terrible must have happened to Ivan. Her impatience to know had taken over, and desperation tugged at her. Esther would be a voice of reason. In truth, she would likely laugh at her for even asking Jesse to do this.

It only took a few minutes for Collette and *Daed* to be on the road. Esther and the rest of the Stutzman family didn't live far, and in less than half an hour, they were pulling up to their big white house.

4

"I'll wait and make sure it's okay for you to stay tonight," *Daed* told her.

"I'm sure it will be, so I'll tell you *gut* night now. *Denki* for bringing me."

"*Gut* night, Collette. You're a *gut* girl."

Collette leaned over and kissed his bearded cheek then climbed out of the buggy. She scampered to the porch and knocked on the door. Esther's mother Margaret opened the door and after a few words, Collette turned and waved at her father that everything was okay.

Esther joined her mother at the door and welcomed Collette in.

"I thought you were going out with Ivan this evening," Esther said under her breath. "What brings you here?"

"Ivan never showed up, and I'm worried sick," Collette confessed as they walked into the dining room to continue talking privately. "I don't know what has happened, but it must be something awful. I was hoping I might talk Jesse into going to the Yordy place and checking on him for me."

Esther's green eyes softened in sympathy, but she shook her head. "We can ask him, Collette, but as late and as freezing as it is, I don't think he'll do it. I think he's coming down with a cold."

Collette's expression fell and Esther continued, offering a bit of hope. "We'll ask him anyway. Come on, he's in his room."

They went upstairs and Esther knocked on a door at the end of the hall. "Jesse, may Collette and I come in?"

"Sure," a voice called from behind the door. "Come on in."

The girls entered the room and found Jesse propped on his bed reading a book in the lantern light. His sandy hair stood in tufts where he'd been running his hand through it. "Hey, what's going on?"

"I wanted to ask you a favor, Jesse," Collette said then explained what she wanted.

"I would, Collette, but goodness, it is late and cold. I'm really not feeling up to it tonight. What if I go first thing in the morning?"

Collette's shoulders drooped with disappointment, but she nodded. If something terrible had happened, she guessed they'd hear soon enough.

"Come on, Collette. We've got some chocolate chip cookies *Mamm* made today. Let's go get some."

Collette and Esther sat at the table and indulged themselves with cookies and milk. Esther chattered away, and Collette responded to her comments. Her mind, however, was not on the conversation.

She couldn't get Ivan out of her head. She'd known him for a long time and looked at him with a bit of hero-worship, she supposed. When she was twelve and he was thirteen, they'd been walking home from school with some of the other kids. Collette was closest to the road when a car came roaring around the corner headed straight toward her. She'd stood there frozen with fear when Ivan leapt over and pushed her out of the car's path. They both rolled down the ditch, and Ivan broke his leg in the fall. Ever since then, Collette had looked on him as her personal hero.

He had never before failed to show up when he said he would. He'd been late sometimes but to just not come? That had never happened. She couldn't ignore the gnawing worry that ate at her.

"Yoo-hoo, Collette. I'm talking to you." Esther tapped Collette's arm. "I asked you if you wanted more cookies."

"I'm sorry, Esther. I just can't stop worrying about Ivan. This just isn't like him."

"Put it in the hands of *Gott*, Collette. He'll watch over Ivan."

"I know. You're right. Worry never accomplishes anything." She was going to try not to think about it anymore tonight.

But that was easier said than done, she thought as she helped Esther wash out the cups and saucers they had used. She swept the floor while Esther wiped down the table and countertops, and she didn't say any more about Ivan before they went up to bed.

But that didn't stop her mind from fretting.

Chapter Two

Collette didn't sleep well that night which didn't surprise her. When she did sleep, she dreamt of hearing terrible news, and she woke up with tangled sheets and a pounding heart.

She got up early and left Esther sleeping, creeping downstairs to make some coffee. She tried to move quietly, but her aunt soon joined her.

"I'm sorry I woke you, *Aenti* Margaret," Collette said as she poured them each a cup of the hot, strong liquid.

"Don't be silly, child. I always get up early. The rest of the family will be along soon. You know we're all early risers. What got you up so early?"

"I just woke up," Collette lied, not wanting to talk about Ivan. "How can I help with breakfast?"

"Would you mind gathering the eggs? It's cold out there, you know, so there won't be many."

"I'll get my coat and go do that."

The cold took Collette's breath away when she stepped outside the door. At least the wind was still, she thought as she watched her breath crystalize in the air. She hurried toward the chicken coop and let herself into the tiny building.

The soft ruffle of feathers greeted her as she tossed down food and went from nest to nest to gather what eggs there were. She placed each one into the basket over her arm then murmured a bit to the chickens, bidding them a good day. She stepped out the door and was startled to see a buggy rolling up the drive.

Her hand flew to her chest. Was it Ivan...or someone bringing news of him? She held her breath until the buggy rolled to a stop and a man climbed out.

She recognized Colin Fischer, Jesse's best friend. Was he the bearer of bad tidings?

"Colin? What is it? Do you have news?" Collette rushed to him. Her knees trembled and her fingers shook when she reached toward him.

Colin looked startled when she ran up to him. "Collette? I didn't know you were here. Is something wrong? News about what?"

Collette sagged with relief. He wasn't here to tell her Ivan had been killed or hurt.

"*Nee, jah*... I don't know." Collette knew she sounded like an idiot, but she was flustered. Colin's appearance was unexpected and the sight of him made her mind flash to the worst-case scenarios. "I don't know. It's just that Ivan and I were supposed to go out last evening, but he never showed

9

up. I came over last night to ask Jesse to go to his house and check on him for me, but Jesse wasn't feeling well. He said he'd go this morning."

"Jesse and I planned on going to the auction in town this morning, but we can go past Ivan's house before we go. The auction doesn't start until ten."

"Would you? That would be wonderful *gut*," Collette said with relief. "I've been worried. He's always been on time before, but last night he just didn't show up."

"I'm sure there's been some kind of misunderstanding. Don't worry." Colin smiled encouragingly at her, and Collette felt her nerves settle a bit. Colin had a way of always making her feel better.

"Come on, let's get those eggs in the house for breakfast, then Jesse and I can get on the road."

Colin flicked the reins and set the buggy in motion. Jesse sat on the seat next to him, still stretching and yawning. It wasn't really all that early anymore as they headed to Ivan Yordy's house.

"I wonder what did happen to Ivan last night," Colin mused as they rode along. "Collette said he's always been reliable before."

"*Jah*, I s'pose," Jesse agreed. "In truth, Ivan's never been my favorite person. I reckon I shouldn't admit that, but there it is."

"Still, he made an obligation to Collette. He should have kept it if he was able." Colin's jaw firmed with his conviction. Ivan wasn't his favorite person, either, but he was a solid enough person. The truth was, Colin had a soft spot for Collette and didn't appreciate anyone making her upset.

"I guess we'll just have to wait and see what his excuse is," Jesse said. "I hope he's got a *gut* one."

"Me, too," Colin agreed and urged the horse to go a little faster.

Fifteen minutes later, they pulled into the Ivan's drive and got out of the buggy. Colin rapped on the front door and soon it was opened by Adele Yordy, Ivan's mother.

"Hello, Mrs. Yordy," Colin said. "We've come to check on Ivan. Is he here?"

Mrs. Yordy's eyes widened. "Why, no, he's not. Is something wrong? Has something happened?"

Jesse explained that Ivan had been expected at his house the evening before, and they were worried because Ivan hadn't shown up.

"Oh, my, he must have forgotten all about it. He went to Yellow Creek yesterday. He was going to stay with his cousin Adam. He may not be back until tomorrow."

Colin kept his face expressionless during the conversation with Mrs. Yordy, but when he climbed back into the buggy, his jaw tightened.

"Well, I guess Ivan had a memory lapse or something," Jesse said, as if attempting to calm Colin down.

"Memory lapse, my eye," Colin grumbled. "He made a promise to Colette, and he broke it. Not *gut*."

"I know it's not *gut*, but it was probably just a slip-up. He's only human, you know."

"He needs to think of other people's feelings. Collette was worried sick." Colin ground out the words. "I bet she hardly slept all night."

Jesse eyed him, a slight twinkle appearing in his eye. "Sounds to me like *you're* worried sick now about my little cousin."

Colin sat up straighter and shook his head. "*Nee.* It just makes me angry when people are rude and thoughtless."

"Well, no denying it was rude all right. But Collette will be happy that's all it was, and Ivan wasn't hurt in any way."

"I don't understand her big attraction for Ivan Yordy in the first place." Colin shook his head.

"Well, love moves in mysterious ways," Jesse said, clearly watching for Colin's reaction. He grinned as his friend gave an angry snort.

"I guess," was all Colin said, shaking his head again. "I'll never understand it."

Jesse laughed out loud. "Looks to me like you might know something about it. I think you have a crush on my cousin."

"I don't," Colin shot back. "I just don't like to see her upset, is all."

"Okay, friend, if you say so."

Colin shot him an angry glare. "Well, I do say so and that's the end of this conversation."

Jesse smothered a smile and refrained from answering back. Colin ground his teeth. Jesse was right. He was acting like a fool—a love-sick fool. What was the matter with him? Yes, he'd always liked Collette, and maybe he'd always felt protective of her. But even he had to admit that his reaction to Ivan's rudeness seemed all out of proportion.

Chapter Three

Colette clutched the potted plant Ivan had presented her with as an apology. He'd come over that afternoon and begged her forgiveness.

"I'm so sorry, Collette. I don't know how I forgot our date. When I saw Adam, and he asked me to come and give him a hand with his work, everything else just flew out of my head. He needed me, and I went. I can't believe I forgot about you." Ivan's big, blue eyes flashed at her. "Please forgive me."

Collette looked at him from under lowered lashes. She knew she should be a little harder on him, but she was so relieved he was all right, she couldn't do it. She certainly didn't like the fact that he'd found her so easy to forget, or that he'd caused her to worry all night, but still... He was so handsome, she couldn't resist his apology.

"Of course, I forgive you. I was so worried something had happened to you." They were standing on the porch of Collette's house. It was uncomfortable out there, as the cold bit at her nose and cheeks, but it wasn't customary to invite a beau inside. The fact that everyone knew they were courting was already more than usual.

Jesse and Colin had brought her word yesterday of Ivan's whereabouts, and that had completely eased her worry. But though she had stopped worrying, and though she did forgive him, it bothered her. Not that she wanted it to. But her mind kept circling. And the more it circled, the more it came up with things that were concerning. Sometimes it seemed like Ivan was thoughtless of others. Oh, nothing big, just in little things, like letting the screen door slam in someone's face or taking the last piece of pie without asking if anyone else wanted it.

But now that Ivan was smiling his dimpled grin at her, she relaxed. Wasn't the Amish way of life all about forgiving and forgetting? And more than anything, she wanted to be pleasing to God. And pleasing to Ivan. He didn't do these things intentionally, she was sure.

Ivan's eyes were unwavering on hers. "I'm glad I'm forgiven. I would hate it if you were angry with me. Now, how about we take a buggy ride and get some fresh air?"

There was nothing she'd like more. "All right," she said. "Let me get my coat."

Collette hurried inside, dropping her shawl on a rocker. In the washroom, she wrapped up in her warm coat and added her outer bonnet, then she told her parents she was leaving. Soon, she and Ivan were in Ivan's buggy trotting down the road that had recently been cleared by the *Englisch*.

Collette sighed contentedly as she settled into the seat. It was one of the coldest days that winter, but yet very beautiful. Fat, fluffy snowflakes drifted across a world cloaked in white. The stark black outline of the trees was softened by the falling snow and Collette felt at peace.

They talked about insignificant things as they rolled along, enjoying the stark countryside. Collette laughed and pointed out a deer leaping across a field, its tail pointing skyward.

"It's so graceful," she breathed.

"*Jah*," Ivan agreed casually. "It would look good on my dinner table."

"Ivan, how can you say that? It's a beautiful, lovely creature."

"It is, and *Gott* put it here for *gut* eating for his people."

"Okay, venison is delicious, but can't you appreciate the beauty of the animal as well?"

"*Jah*, I s'pose."

"I think it's lovely." She played with the strings of her outer bonnet and changed the subject. "So some of us are getting together Friday night to plan a little something for the district youth for Valentine's Day. We're not supposed to call it Valentine's Day, by the way. I s'pose that's too worldly. When we talked to the deacon, he suggested we call it something else, so no one gets offended by us celebrating what's considered an *Englisch* holiday. You'll come, won't you?"

Ivan looked away before answering her. "I don't know, Collette. I kind of promised Adam I'd come back and help him with that project he's working on."

"What *is* he working on?" she asked, tilting her head and looking at him.

"Oh, you know, some stuff around his house." He looked away from her, and Collette felt an uneasiness tease her—why, she couldn't imagine.

"I see. You couldn't go over Saturday morning instead?"

"*Nee.* I told him Friday. That way, we can get an early start Saturday."

"I see. Well, I can drive myself, I guess. The meeting's going to be at the Kraus's house. That's not far at all."

"Sure. And just because I can't make the meeting, doesn't mean I don't want to be involved."

"Okay, *gut.* I'll tell you what decisions we make when you get back."

"Sounds fine. Now, I should get you home."

Collette wasn't in any rush, but she didn't say anything. In truth, it was getting dark and the snow hadn't stopped falling.

"Okay. I'm glad you came by this afternoon."

"I had to. I had to apologize to you." Ivan looked at her with serious eyes. "I *am* sorry, you know. I should have been there. After all, you are hard to forget. I don't know how I managed it."

Color stained her cheeks as she looked down at her mittened hands. If she was so hard to forget, how come he had done so? Well, she wasn't going to hold a grudge. Instead, she smiled and let his words warm her heart.

Colin ran the brush down Thunder's flank. The horse stood patiently as Colin brushed him, enjoying the attention.

"Ah, Thunder, you don't know how *gut* you have it. You're a gelding. You don't have to worry about girl problems." Colin shook his head. "I wish I didn't have to, either." He snorted, amused that he was talking about this to his horse. Still, who else would he want to tell? "Unfortunately for me, I've gone and fallen for a woman who loves another man."

Colin straightened and scratched his head, ruffling the sable curls along his neck. He hadn't wanted to admit it, not even to himself, but it was true. He was in love with Colette Bontrager, and she was in love with Ivan Yordy.

He didn't know how it had sneaked up on him. He'd moved here to Baker's Corner a few years before from Ohio when his uncle had offered him a position with his company renovating houses. And Colin had grown fond of the area. He had immediately become good friends with Jesse Stutzman, and they often spent time together fishing or doing chores. Jesse worked for Amos, too. Through Jesse, Colin had met Collette.

The memory of that first meeting brought a smile to his face. Collette had been at Jesse's house visiting her cousins, and Colin had come by to pick Jesse up to go to a ball game. Esther had been standing at the base of a big tree when he rolled up.

"Hi, Esther. What's up?"

"My friend Collette, that's what's up." She pointed up the trunk of the tree. Colin looked up and spotted the face of an angel staring down at him. Her hair was golden-red and tiny wisps escaped from under her *kapp* to frame her face.

"Well, hello," he called up. "What are you doing up there?"

"I'm rescuing a kitten who ran up to save himself from a dog, but now he doesn't know how to get down." She held up a tiny black and white kitten where she sat on a limb. "Here, catch."

Colin had jerked with reaction and caught the furry little bundle she'd tossed ever-so-gently to him. He held the kitten close and comforted it as the slender girl shimmied down from the tree.

"Thanks. The poor little thing was terrified, his heart beating like a baby bird's. I wasn't sure how I was going to hold him and climb down at the same time. You're tall enough that you could catch him easily. By the way, I'm Collette Bontrager. You must be Colin. Jesse said you'd be here soon."

He was overwhelmed by her melodious chatter. In truth, Collette Bontrager was like a force, pressing into him with her beauty. She brought something out in him that he'd never even knew was there.

"*Jah*, I'm Colin Fischer. I must say, you are the prettiest nut in this oak tree." He couldn't help it. He knew it was a little forward, but he meant it. She was beautiful with her big, green eyes and freckled nose. She was petite and slender and the forest green dress she wore brought out the color of her eyes. She had an impish grin that made her face completely charming.

He'd only grown fonder of her since then. Not only was she attractive; she was a good, kind person. She worked in her father's small store and was always going out of her way to help people. He knew she made deliveries to homebound customers at no extra charge. She also helped with church activities, and she assisted folks who were sick.

She had a big heart; he knew that, and she was almost always happy.

But he'd never gone after her, a fact he now regretted. He'd made one excuse after another, mainly because he somehow thought it might interfere with his friendship with Jesse. For what would happen if something went sour between him and Collette? Wouldn't that be awkward with Jesse?

As he thought about it now, he realized he'd been a fool. And then, it'd been too late. Collette and Ivan were courting. He'd known about it before everyone else, for Esther had let it slip. His heart had plunged at the news, and it was then that he realized he'd missed his chance. Since then, he'd denied anything he felt for her. Denied it to himself and to everyone else.

Well, he couldn't deny it any longer.

In truth, he felt like really giving it to Ivan. His people didn't believe in violence, but he found himself feeling downright angry for the way Ivan treated her. He'd hated seeing her pale face and her worried eyes. Then to find out Ivan had just forgotten all about her and gone on his merry way...? Colin always tried to control his temper, but at that moment he'd wanted to punch Ivan. He knew those feelings were wrong, even sinful, but there it was.

He tried to tell himself that it really wasn't any of his business. He had no claims on Collette, thanks to his own stupidity. He had to harden his heart against the protective, possessive feelings she aroused in him. Collette was an adult. She had made her choice.

Chapter Four

Charlotte Kraus swung open the front door and greeted Collette, Esther, and Jesse. The three had arrived simultaneously and were all standing on the porch.

"Hello, hello, come in out of the cold. Let me take your coats." The brown-headed woman ushered them into her home and said, "The others are in the dining room."

Collette walked in and saw Colin, Charlotte's brother-in-law, Leon Kraus, and Heidi Kaufman at the table. Charlotte's husband Michael was just coming in from the kitchen and urged them to have a seat. It was kind of both Charlotte and Michael to help out with the youth events, as usually once a person was married, they were no longer involved.

"So, I guess we're all here now. Let's talk about what we want to do for the youth for Valentine's Day."

"We want to have fun, we know that. How about a games night?" Collette asked.

"That sounds *gut*. We all like games," Heidi agreed.

"I know we had one a few months ago, but I think enough time has passed. Besides, most of us wouldn't mind having one every month," Collette added.

"Okay, then a games night it is. Everyone agree?" Michael asked. A murmur of consent went around the table.

"What games should we play?" Michael asked.

The discussion grew lively as they tossed around suggestions and remembered the other fun game nights they had participated in.

"Remember the night we had a games night at the Yordy house?" Leon asked. "Ivan got so enthusiastic playing Spoons that he knocked over the whole table."

"It wasn't his fault," Collette jumped in to defend the absent Ivan. "He caught his foot on his chair leg, and it made him jerk and fall."

"Sure, sure, but it was funny." Leon chuckled then took another sip of coffee before saying, "By the way, where is Ivan tonight? I figured he'd be here with us." He gave Collette a meaningful look.

Collette tried to answer casually. "He's in Yellow Creek helping his cousin."

"In Yellow Creek again, huh?" Jessie questioned. "What are they working on, Collette? It must be something big to go for two weeks in a row."

"I don't know. He didn't say," she answered quietly then quickly changed the subject. "Say, we need to decide where the game night will take place. Any volunteers?"

"Why not here?" Charlotte asked. "This old house is huge. There's plenty of room. The house had been added on to a dozen times over the years."

They all agreed the Kraus house would be the perfect location, then moved on to discuss other things. They decided there would be ice skating earlier in the evening if the Lapp pond was still frozen over—which it was certainly expected to be, and then they talked about refreshments.

Well into the discussion, Charlotte called for a break so they could indulge in the pecan pies she'd made for the occasion. She served hearty slices and talk almost ceased as they enjoyed the delicious dessert.

Collette finished her piece and leaned back and groaned, patting her belly. "That was absolutely scrumptious, Charlotte.

"*Denki*, Collette. It was made from my *grossmammi's* recipe."

"Well, it was wonderful *gut*. I'm going to take my plate to the kitchen. Anyone else ready? I'll take yours, too."

She gathered up several plates, but Colin waved her off with a grin. "I've still got a couple of bites left. I'm not giving it up until every bite is gone."

"I don't blame you," Collette said as she headed to the kitchen. She put the plates and forks into the sink and started the water running. She might as well wash the dishes up while she was right here.

She had almost finished with the few saucers when Colin walked in and handed her his fork and plate. "Did you drive over alone, Collette?"

"*Jah*. It's just a couple of miles down the road, you know."

23

"I know. I don't like that you're out alone on a cold night like this, though."

She turned wide eyes on him. "Colin, I'm a big girl. I can take care of myself."

Colin nodded. "Of course, you can. I just wish you didn't have to."

Collette laughed lightly. "I'll be fine. I reckon you drove alone?" she asked, teasing.

He gave her a smile. "That I did. But it's cold and dark tonight. I'll follow you home to make sure you get there okay, if you'd like."

"*Nee*, Colin, you live the complete other direction. I'll be fine on my own."

He gave in reluctantly. "But it wouldn't be any trouble."

She turned and smiled at him. "*Denki*, Colin, but people might get the wrong idea if I let you follow me. You know, they might talk." She was only too aware of how tongues in their district liked to wag. And now that most folks knew she and Ivan were courting, Colin's attention wouldn't go unnoticed.

"We wouldn't have to announce it," he countered.

"*Nee*. Truly, it's fine. Besides, I don't think Ivan would like it," she said. She'd already seen a bit of Ivan's jealous side.

"I guess Ivan should have been here then," Colin retorted then turned and left the room.

Collette's eyes widened at Colin's rather sharp tone. She'd never seen the good-natured man get cross before. And over this? She shook her head in wonder. He almost acted as if he cared for her. Well, of course, he cared for her—they were friends, after all. And her cousin was his best friend. But this had seemed like more than that.

She laughed at herself. She was being silly. Colin had never had feelings for her other than friendship...had he?

Collette spent the next day working at her father's specialty store at the edge of town. It was demanding, for the store was popular with both Amish and *Englisch*. She was kept busy slicing lunch meats and cheeses, and packaging cookies and candies. Sometimes she spent the day baking but not that day. Amelia, who usually worked the counter, had called in sick, so Collette took her place.

She had just finished slicing a pound of ham when she looked up and saw Esther in her line.

"Hello, Esther. What brings you out today?"

"Hello, Collette. *Mamm* wants some corned beef. She's going to make Ruebens for supper. Doesn't that sound yummy?"

"Oh, it does. Maybe I should spend the night with you tonight." Collette laughed.

"Why don't you? You can go home after preaching service tomorrow."

"I'd love to, but it is your turn to spend the night at my house you know. I stayed at yours last time."

"But we're having Ruebens..." Esther said in a cajoling voice.

Collette laughed again. "All right. Who can say no to a *gut* Rueben sandwich? I'll be there after work."

Esther nodded. "Now, how about some cheese to go with the meat?"

~

Daed pulled up in front of the Stutzman's house later that afternoon. It was Saturday, so they had closed at three o'clock. Earlier, they'd stopped by the house so Collette could get her things and could tell her mother her plans before heading over to her cousin's home.

"I'll see you at preaching service tomorrow, *Daed*," Collette said as she hopped out of the buggy at her cousins' house.

He waved goodbye and rolled down the drive as Esther opened the door to her.

"Hi. Come on in. We've started making the sandwiches. You can help."

"I would love to." She walked into the kitchen and greeted Aunt Margaret. Soon, they were all busy making sandwiches. Collette got out some macaroni salad and dill pickle spears from the refrigerator.

"It looks delicious," Colette said as Margaret added sauerkraut to the sandwiches. "Are we about ready?"

"I think we are. John, run out to the barn and get Jesse and Colin, please," Margaret told her younger son. "Tell them supper's ready."

"Oh, I didn't know Colin was here," Collette said in a startled voice.

"*Jah*, I forgot to tell you. He and Jesse are working on sharpening tools in the barn. They've been at it for hours."

Collette didn't know why her stomach did a flip just then. She'd always been comfortable around Colin. Why did the thought of his presence disturb her lately?

"Come on, let's get the food on the table. Everyone is hungry, or at least, I know I am. My stomach is growling," Esther said.

"We'd better get you fed then," Collette said, laughing at her cousin. "We wouldn't want you to miss a meal."

"Who's going to miss a meal?" Colin inquired as the two men came into the kitchen. "Not me, I hope."

"*Nee*, not you." Esther chuckled. "In fact, if you get washed up, we can eat."

A few minutes later, they sat down at the table and had the silent blessing. Then the feast was on. Colette loved the tangy sandwich and the cool macaroni salad. She especially enjoyed the dill pickles.

After supper was finished, the girls cleaned up then rounded up the others so they could play Yahtzee. They sat around the dining room table and began rolling the dice. Soon the guys were cracking jokes. They laughed so much, Collette was grasping her ribs and gasping for air before they finally wound down.

The rest of the family each said their good-nights as they wandered off to bed, and soon there was only Colin, Collette, Jesse and Esther left downstairs.

"Say, why don't we build the fire up in the fireplace and make some s'mores?" Esther suggested.

"Mmm, that sounds yummy," Colette agreed.

"I'm in," Colin said.

Colin and Jesse worked on getting the fire to burn brighter, and Colette and Esther went to the kitchen and gathered the ingredients. Esther dug out the skewers they used to cook hotdogs over the fire outside, and in a few minutes, they all settled down on the floor in front of the fireplace and roasted marshmallows.

They put together the concoctions and indulged. Collette moaned with delight as she licked the sticky goo from her fingers.

She looked up just in time to meet Colin's gaze. The look on his face made her heart beat faster. Why was he staring at her like she was the edible treat instead of the s'more in his hand? A shiver slid down her spine as their gazes remained locked for a long moment.

She broke eye contact first, and a moment later, Colin said he should probably be going.

Chapter Five

There was another meeting about the Valentine's Day game night to decide on the decorations they would use. Of course, they had to be sparse, but they could still be colorful and festive—if understated.

They concluded that red candles, red paper plates and cups, and white tablecloths would work nicely. Esther was in charge of getting supplies for the party and headed into town one afternoon to get them.

She was enjoying looking around the store at the variety of decorations and silk flowers available. She had just plucked up a bunch of artificial roses when she overheard some talk from the next aisle.

"*Jah*, she said it's Ivan Yordy."

The words caught Esther's attention, and she listened more intently. She felt a bit guilty to be purposefully eavesdropping, but she excused herself by rationalizing that she owed it to her cousin to hear what was being said.

"My niece Iris said that's who is courting her. Of course, he's from here in Baker's Point, and she lives in Yellow Creek. Do you know him?" the first woman's voice asked.

"I know some of the Yordy family, but I'm not sure about Ivan. He must be one of Carl Yordy's boys," another voice said.

"My niece seems to really like him," the first voice confided. "She said he's nice and steady and could provide a *gut* home."

The voices faded away as the women moved off. Esther stood there with shock running through her. Ivan? *Collette's* Ivan? Courting some other girl?

Surely, she had misunderstood.

But no, Esther knew what she had heard, and the woman distinctly named Ivan Yordy. It had to be Collette's Ivan because Esther seriously doubted there were two of them living here in Baker's Point.

Should she tell Collette what she had heard? It would upset her terribly if she thought Ivan was two-timing her.

But wouldn't it be better if Collette knew the truth? She deserved a beau who would be honest with her, not someone who lied to her and snuck around behind her back.

Esther would have to tell her cousin what she'd head. She hated to be the one to do it, but it had to be done. Determined, she took her purchases to the clerk and checked out.

∾

Colette wiped down the counter where she had just finished making refrigerator cookie dough. She would come in to work bright and early tomorrow and get them in the oven.

"Hi, Collette. Are you busy?"

Collette looked up to see Esther standing in the kitchen doorway. "Hi. *Nee*, I'm not. As a matter of fact, I just finished up for the day. Why? What's up?"

"Um, not much... If you're done, why don't we go get a cup of coffee at the café? I've got the buggy outside."

"Okay. Let me get my coat and tell *Daed* where I'm going."

Collette didn't take long to get ready. Ten minutes later, they were settling into a booth at the café and placing their orders.

"I got the candles and supplies for game night," Esther said, her fingers plucking at the tablecloth. "I also got some white paper doilies and red construction paper so we can make hearts and paper chains. We can even make some Valentine cards..."

"*Ach,* that might be fun," Collette said.

"While I was there—at the shop, I overheard something that disturbed me a little." Esther glanced at her nervously.

"Well, don't stop now, Esther. Tell me what you heard."

"I heard ... one woman telling another woman that her niece was being courted by Ivan Yordy." The words rushed out and she braced herself for Collette's response.

At first, Collette didn't say a word. She stopped stirring her coffee and remained motionless for a long moment. At last, she spoke very quietly.

"Ivan? Are you sure it was *Ivan* Yordy? He has several brothers, you know."

"I know, so I listened very carefully, and they said his name again. It was Ivan."

Collette frowned. Surely, Esther had misunderstood. Ivan would never do that. He'd practically proposed to her already. She was hoping he would do it officially on Valentine's Day. He wouldn't be seeing another woman if he was planning on marrying her.

She shook her head. "*Nee.* I don't believe it. He wouldn't do that to me."

"I hope not, Collette. I hope there is some misunderstanding. The other girl is supposedly from Yellow Creek."

Collette's breath stopped. "*Yellow Creek? Nee. Nee.* There must be a misunderstanding. I'm seeing him tomorrow night. I'm going to ask him about it."

"I think you should."

Collette nodded in agreement. "I am definitely going to talk to him about it. There is surely some explanation."

Please, she prayed, her stomach twisting in knots. *Let him have a reasonable explanation.*

Ivan picked Collette up the next night and took her to a birthday gathering for her friend Sarah. At first, Collette didn't say anything about the rumor she'd heard. She wanted them to enjoy the evening without any tension between them, so she stayed silent on the subject until after the party.

On the way home, however, she brought the subject up. "Ivan, I need to talk to you about something."

"I thought something was bothering you. You've been quiet all evening. What is it?" He looked over at her, his expression curious.

"Someone overheard some talk about you. It seems some woman was telling another woman that you are courting her niece."

"What? I'm courting her niece? Who's niece?"

"That's what was said." Collette drew in a deep breath and looked steadily at him. "Are you?"

"Collette, h-how could you ask me that? I've been courting you for a long time now. You know how I feel about you."

Collette lowered her gaze and looked at her hands. "I asked if they were sure they heard your name, and they said they were."

"Don't you trust me, Collette?" he implored, his tone offended. "That hurts my feelings, you know."

Collette looked at him then. His eyes were clear, and his expression was intent. He looked innocent. Guilt swirled through her. How could she suspect her own beau of such a thing? Esther had to have been mistaken. Or those women who were talking—they were the ones who'd gotten Ivan's name wrong.

Or maybe... Could Esther be trying to break her and Ivan up? After all, Esther didn't have a beau of her own. Maybe she didn't want Collette to have one either.

She shuddered. *Ach*, where her mind was going... That was not possible. Esther was her dear cousin; she wasn't that type of person. More guilt flooded Collette for her suspicious thoughts.

But who was telling her the truth? Was Ivan?

"I'm sure it must have been a misunderstanding," she finally said, determined not to let this damage her relationship with either her cousin or Ivan.

"It must be," Ivan insisted. "You know you have my heart."

Collette drew in a deep breath and closed her eyes. His words made her feel better, but for some reason, there was still a hollow feeling in the pit of her stomach.

Chapter Six

Collette peeled potatoes for supper while her mother checked on the meatloaf in the oven. Collette tried to focus on what her mother was saying to her, but her mind kept drifting.

"I said, how are the plans for the game night coming?" Dorothy asked for the second time.

"*Ach,* sorry, *Mamm,* I guess I was wool-gathering." Collette picked up another potato. "Everything is going pretty well, I s'pose. We're going ice skating first, then we've got all kinds of games planned – Life on the Farm, Sorry, Yahtzee, Monopoly, Scrabble, just to name a few. We'll gather them from folks who will let us use them."

"It sounds like fun. I suppose you'll be going with Ivan," Dorothy said.

"*Jah,* probably," she said uncertainly. After all that had happened, she wasn't sure she trusted Ivan right now. He had denied seeing the other girl in Yellow Creek, but as time went on, she had her doubts. He had been going to Yellow Creek frequently lately.

"You sound a bit uncertain, Collette. Is something wrong?" Dorothy sat down at the kitchen table and looked at her daughter. She had six older children and had been through a myriad of ups and downs with them; Collette knew her mother could tell when one of her children was troubled.

Collette hesitated then began to tell her mother what Esther had told her. Soon the words were tumbling out of her, and she was revealing her worries, the potato in her hand all but forgotten.

"I don't know what to do, *Mamm*," she admitted, blinking back tears. "The accusations are really just hearsay, but Ivan is acting a bit suspiciously, too."

Dorothy reached over and covered Collette's hand with her own. "Listen to your heart, *dochder*," she said. "Let *Gott* speak to your heart and trust what you hear."

Collette looked at her mother and drew in a shuddering breath. "That's the problem. My heart is telling me two different things."

"Now, it is. The message isn't clear yet. Soon, though, you'll learn the language of your heart, and then you'll know what to do."

"I pray you're right, *Mamm*," Collette whispered. "I pray you're right."

"Give it time, *dochder*. I think you'll see I am."

Colin handed Jesse a hammer and watched as Jesse pounded a nail. They were replacing the older steps to the hayloft in the Stutzmans' barn to ensure they were strong and safe. They had been working at it for a while now, and they were nearly finished.

"One more to go after this one," Colin commented. "Then we can go get something to eat."

"Sounds good. I'm so hungry I could eat your cooking," Jesse joked.

"Hey, it's not that bad. You ate that chili I made the other day."

"Okay, I'll give you that. You do make a decent pot of chili. You know who really makes good chili, though?" He paused but didn't wait for an answer. "Collette."

"That doesn't surprise me. She does a lot of cooking at their store. You've probably had her cinnamon rolls, haven't you? Mmm, heavenly."

"She is a *gut* cook. Did I tell you what Esther told me?" Jesse cocked his head over his shoulder and looked at Colin.

"*Nee.* What?" Colin picked up the last step he had cut for the ladder.

"She overheard a woman in the store saying her niece from Yellow Creek was being courted by Ivan Yordy."

"Whoa. When was this?" Colin straightened, his face taking on a stony expression.

"A couple of days ago. Esther said she didn't see the woman, she was in the next aisle, but she said she heard her clearly."

A spark of anger lit deep in Colin's stomach. Was Ivan Yordy *cheating* on Collette? No, surely, he wasn't that stupid. Colette was so sweet and pretty, any man who won her heart would be a fool to risk losing her.

"I don't believe it," Colin said under his breath.

"That's what Esther said Collette told her, too. She refused to believe it, but said she was going to talk to Ivan about it."

"Will he tell her the truth, I wonder?" Colin said. "She's innocent enough to believe him even if it isn't true."

"She trusts way too easy," Jesse agreed.

"That's because she has a sweet, pure soul, untainted by lies and hate."

Jesse glanced up at him and shook his head, as if acknowledging that Colin had it bad.

"What are you smiling at? You know it's true."

"*Jah*, it's true, but I'm shaking my head at you. You are Collette's number one fan, aren't you? When are you going to do something about it?"

"I think she's fine, if that's what you mean," Colin said defensively, basically ignoring Jesse's question.

Jesse sighed. "I've never been a big fan of Ivan Yordy, as you know."

"Well, apparently Collette is, and that's the problem."

Jesse ran his hand through his hair. "Maybe, she'll see the light before it's too late."

"I hope so. She's too sweet a girl to be hurt by a two-timer."

"*Jah*, she is. Maybe you can help her change her mind, my friend."

Colin sighed and shifted his weight from one foot to the other. "I ain't sure how I'd do that."

"Maybe you won't have to. Maybe Ivan will tell her the truth...or maybe he'll mess up and get caught."

"I wonder if she would break up with him even if she caught him red-handed," Colin said. "She seems blind to any faults he might have."

"One time I criticized him for bad table manners, and Collette flew to his defense. I've been more careful after that..."

"Well, they say love is blind. I guess in this case, it must be true."

"I would hate to see my little cousin brokenhearted, but if he is cheating on her, she better discover the truth before they marry. If he cheats now, he might be willing to do it after they are wed. And then, she'll be trapped."

Colin nodded. "Collette would be miserable if she wound up married to a man who cheated on her. I pray to *Gott* He protects her from that. I... I will think on it. I could try to step in."

"Be careful. That could go sour on you right easy. Well, I think we're done here. Let's go eat."

Colin followed Jesse into the house, but he had trouble getting his mind off Collette.

Chapter Seven

Collette had the afternoon off from work and decided she'd go to the city's public library before she went home. She loved to read, but unfortunately didn't get much time to indulge in the pleasure. She did want to pick up a couple of books, though. The weather was conducive to reading with its short hours of light and frequent snowfalls.

She liked a variety of genres when it came to books. She liked biographies, books about animals, and mysteries. She read about other religions and other lands. Her taste was quite eclectic.

She roamed the quiet book stacks, looking to find something that caught her attention. She loved being in the library. It was peaceful and nearly silent, and her parents had never forbid her from using the library. She knew that not all folks in their district were in favor of it, but her parents always allowed her—if she was careful with her book selections.

The other clients sat and read, worked on the computers, or, like her, roved between the tall shelves filled with books. In her mind, the books contained tickets to the world, books that could transport her to secret lands and fairy tales.

Collette thumbed through a coffee table book that featured photos of the Rocky Mountains and some of its native habitats. She was awed by the towering summits and the deer drinking from the crystal clear lake. Maybe someday she could see it for herself.

"Beautiful, *ain't so?*"

The deep voice coming from behind her startled Collette so badly she jerked and dropped the book. The loud boom it made when it hit the floor drew every gaze in the place as she turned and confronted Colin.

"Colin, you scared me near to death," she whispered hotly, her cheeks flaming.

"I'm sorry, Collette. I didn't mean to," he apologized. "I saw you through the window when I was going to lunch. I wondered if you might want to join me. My treat."

The invitation took Collette by surprise. She had no real reason to say no, and just as she was considering it, her stomach let out an audible growl. Her eyes widened and her hand flew to lay across her flat belly.

Colin laughed and said, "Well, that settles it. You're definitely hungry, so we will go to lunch. Are you ready to check out?"

"*Jah*, I s'pose so." She clutched the two books she was holding close to her chest so he couldn't see the titles. Today, she had decided on a couple of Amish romances, but she didn't want him to know that.

They moved to the desk and Collette handed the books to the librarian who smiled warmly at her, scanned the titles,

41

and handed them back. Then she and Colin turned and walked out of the library.

"Is Mary's Café all right with you?" Colin asked as they emerged into the bright daylight.

"That suits."

They entered the small Amish-run café and found seats at a booth. Collette picked up the menu and studied it, avoiding Colin's eyes. He'd never asked her to lunch before and she had an uneasy feeling in the pit of her stomach. Of course, she didn't consider this a date, as that would be inappropriate. It was simply two friends eating together.

A plump, older woman came over and greeted them and put two glasses of water on the table. Collette ordered broccoli-cheese soup and Colin ordered a cheeseburger and fries. Then the woman was gone, and they were alone again.

"The weather's been *gut* the past couple of days, *ain't so?*" she asked, grasping for something to say.

"Oh, *jah*, very nice. It must be all of thirty degrees today."

"Well, at least it's sunny and not snowing."

"You're right. We can be thankful for that. I can't wait until spring gets here, though."

"Oh, me neither. I love spring. Everything's so fresh and new. There are baby animals and new leaves, and flowers blooming everywhere. It's my favorite time of year."

Colin leaned back in his chair and studied her. She looked pretty with the sunlight pouring in the window and highlighting her cameo-like profile. The hair that wasn't covered by her *kapp* sparkled like a new penny and fine silky wisps had escaped around her face.

He murmured a reply to her comment then continued chatting about inconsequential items until the waitress returned with their food.

"Mmm, this looks *gut*," Collette said.

"I imagine it is because everything they make here is *gut*. Want a French fry?" he offered.

"*Nee, denki*," she said primly. She bit the corner of her lip, though, and he was certain that she was tempted to reach over and grab one.

"Okay. Well, enjoy your soup."

For the next few minutes, they indulged in the tasty food and the occasional tidbit of conversation. When Colin asked her if she and Esther were making food for the game night, she assured him they were.

"So, are you and Ivan going to be there together?" he asked.

"I'm planning on it," she told him. "Are you bringing someone?"

He chuckled and shook his head. "*Nee*. I'm going alone...or with Jesse. Won't he make a nice date?"

"*Jah*, for sure," she said with a grin. "You'll make a charming couple."

He sobered suddenly and pinned her with his gaze. "Is that what you like about Ivan? His charm?"

Collette blushed and took a bite of her soup as if to buy some time before answering. He was dying to know how she'd answer.

"Collette?"

"I don't know, Colin. There are lots of things I like about him. I'll never forget that he saved my life once."

"What happened?"

"A bunch of us kids were walking home from school one day. I was about twelve and acting silly, twirling around and stuff in the middle of the road, when a car came flying around the corner. Ivan jumped out and pushed me out of the way. We both hit the ditch and he broke his leg. If he hadn't done that, I would have been hit."

Colin digested her words, studying her. "So, he's like your knight in shining armor?"

Heat stained her cheeks. He hoped he hadn't sounded begrudging. But how could he compete with someone who had saved her life?

"*Nee*," she answered. "He's just a man, like any other. It's not like I look at him as one of those *Englisch* superheroes or anything."

"Don't you, Collette? It seems like you do sometimes. Would you believe he was doing something wrong if you saw it with your own eyes?" He was pushing her and holding his breath. He prayed this wouldn't backfire.

"Of course, I would. But I won't believe it if the source is just rumors and hearsay."

~

Collette bristled at his words. Had he heard about the woman who claimed Ivan was courting her niece in Yellow Creek? Why was that gossip even circulating?

"You're a very loyal woman, Collette," Colin said quietly. "I hope you don't misplace that loyalty."

Her gaze collided with his, and time seemed to stop for a moment. Her breath caught in her chest and for a minute, she felt like she was drowning in his golden eyes. Suddenly, she needed to get away from him so she could breathe again.

"Well, I-I really must get going. *Denki* for lunch, Colin. It's been a pleasure." With that, she slid out of the booth and into her coat. "I'll see you soon."

"*Gut*-bye, Collette," he said as he waved to the waitress for the bill. "I'll see you Saturday when we go to collect the games people are lending us for games night."

"*Jah*, see you then," she agreed and then hurried to escape as fast as possible.

Chapter Eight

Colin swung the sledgehammer with enthusiasm. It felt good to knock down the wall in the old house they were working on renovating. With every swing of the hammer, he felt better.

He didn't know why he was tense. He shouldn't be. Everything was going well. Work was good, his friends were well, everything was fine.

Yet he still felt like an explosion was building within him. He felt the urge to slam this tool harder and harder into the plaster wall.

"Hey, Colin, take it easy, will ya?" his coworker hollered. "You're hitting that wall so hard, you're going to knock the whole house down. Man, you must be really mad at somebody."

"Sorry," he called back then put the hammer on the floor for a minute. He needed to pause and get ahold of himself. *Lord, help me mind my own business,* he prayed. He had to fight the urge to go find Ivan Yordy and demand to know the truth. If Ivan was cheating on Collette, Colin wanted him to pay.

He was painfully aware that his anger and jealousy were sins, and he hated that he was fighting those emotions. In his gut, he was sure the rumors were true. Why would that woman in the store have said that if it wasn't true? Sure, her niece could have been exaggerating, but he had a feeling she wasn't.

He picked the sledgehammer back up and returned to work on the wall, this time holding back a little on the power he put into the whacks. He was being out-of-line. He had no right to try and control Collette. They were simply friends, no more.

But he hated the thought that Ivan might be taking advantage of her trusting nature. She wasn't the type of person to think someone she cared about would be so deceitful. It would be only too easy to pull the wool over her eyes.

That said a lot about the kind of person Ivan was, Colin thought with disgust. But he shouldn't convict the man without more evidence, he told himself. He had to be patient. Time would show whether his instincts about Ivan were right or wrong. In the meantime, he would keep his eyes and ears open on Collette's behalf.

Collette sat at her desk and thought about the card she was going to make for Ivan for Valentine's Day. She wanted it to be special, to express her feelings for him, as well as her hopes and expectations for their future together.

47

She'd thought about such things for so, so many months now. She daydreamed about the large family they would have together, the way they would work together to make a happy home. He would work as the farmer he was; she would make their food and clothes and keep their house neat and tidy. The children would grow and play and learn, and they would all worship together.

Oh, she knew it wouldn't be a perfect life. There was no such thing. There would be ups and downs, triumphs and defeats, good health, and times of sickness. But they would see it all through together, and that was the important thing. That was what made a marriage strong—to face problems and joys together. With the help and guidance of God, they could thrive.

For a moment, doubt flickered through her mind. Would Ivan live up to the standards she wanted in a husband? Was he mature enough to take on those responsibilities?

Even more importantly, was he being honest with her? Without honesty, she didn't think a marriage could be strong. Honesty was a deciding factor in the character of a man. What if he was lying to her?

No, she refused to believe Ivan was deceiving her. They were too close; they had known each other for too long. They were planning on spending the rest of their lives together.

She drew a notebook toward her so she could work on a poem before she committed to the card stock she had purchased.

She wondered if Ivan would put this much thought and time into creating a card or present for her. It would be so treasured and meaningful if he did.

I bet Colin would.

The thought took her by surprise and shook her to the core. Why on earth was she thinking of Colin when she was in the middle of making a card for the man she loved? She shouldn't even be thinking of Colin at all.

Collette cocked her head as she heard her mother calling for her.

She sighed and lay her pen down and turned her mind away from Ivan Yordy and Colin Fischer. They were giving her a headache anyway.

She went downstairs and found her mother in the kitchen.

"What do you need, *Mamm*?" she asked as she entered the room.

"Ah, there you are, Collette," her mother said. "I wondered if you wanted to try this new brownie recipe. I thought you might like to make them for the games night."

"What's special about these?" She let the chocolatey morsel melt in her mouth.

"They're called chocolate kisses, but you don't have to use that name at the party. We don't want to encourage any shenanigans, you know," Dorothy said with a chuckle.

"They are delicious. And hopefully, we'll be too busy for that," Colette said. Although, it would be nice to steal a kiss from Ivan, though. Or even Colin—

She froze. Once again, she was shocked by her own thoughts. Why was she thinking about kissing that man? They were just friends, and that was all they would ever be. She'd already given her heart to Ivan. She was the one cheating when she allowed thoughts like that to slip into her head. If not literally, then emotionally and mentally.

She didn't like feeling this way. It was like...guilt? But why should she feel guilty just because stray thoughts popped uninvited into her head now and then? After all, she did not have control over involuntary thoughts. She hadn't acted on them, had she?

Had Ivan?

Collette felt guilty for entertaining suspicious thoughts about her beau again. She must stick to her resolution to trust him until she had good reason not to.

Chapter Nine

Colin looked forward to spending the day with Collette as they gathered games to play at games night. It was an unexpected and unusual chance to be alone with her for the entire afternoon, an opportunity to get to know her better.

He whistled as he drove Thunder toward the Bontrager farm. He was in a good mood. The snow was falling gently, and it wasn't too cold. It should make for a pleasant afternoon drive.

He pulled into the driveway and climbed out of the buggy. He strode to the door and knocked. Collette pulled open the door so quickly that he still had his arm raised.

"Well, hello there," he greeted her. "Are you ready to go?"

"I am. Just let me grab these cups of hot mulled cider I have ready for us."

A minute late she appeared bearing two big metal cups of the spicy beverage and handed him one.

"*Denki*, Collette. It smells right tasty." Collin took a sip of the warm cider and sighed with satisfaction. "It's wonderful *gut*."

"*Denki*. I thought it would help keep us warm on our errand. I'm leaving, *Mamm*," she called and went out the door.

Soon the horse was trotting down the road toward the Lapp house. The Lapps were lending them two games for the Valentine's party. They were an older couple whose children were grown but they still enjoyed playing games together with the family.

One of the games they picked up was a trivia game, and when they were back in the buggy, Collette opened the box and pulled out some cards with questions on them.

"Okay, let's get a little practice in," she said with a grin. "What is the loudest animal on earth?"

"I actually know that one. It's the sperm whale." Collin grinned. He enjoyed storing tidbits of odd knowledge and trivia in his mind.

"How in the world did you know that?" Collette asked, her eyes wide.

"I know lots of things. Just ask me." He gave her a cocky smile.

"Well, then, tell me this... What do you call a Japanese-style poem with seventeen syllables?"

"That would be a haiku. Do you haiku?"

Collette managed to maintain a straight face as she replied, "I do. Do you?"

"Me, too," he said then burst into laughter. "We're quite the poets, *ain't so?*"

"We are. Seriously, though, I love haikus, even if most Amish aren't too keen on poetry."

"So, you like it?" he asked.

"*Jah,* I must confess I do. I guess that's why Psalms is my favorite book in the Bible. It's like *Gott's* poetry."

He turned and looked at her, studying her earnest face. "That's a lovely way to put it."

"It's true. So many of the Psalms are like songs of praise, and comfort, and love."

"There are songs of lament, too," he pointed out.

"*Jah,* but all the Psalms are about emotions, whether they are sad, joyful, adoring, or full of gratitude."

"I agree. The Psalms are...whoa, there!" Colin pulled at the reins as a pickup truck swerved toward them, gunning its engine and tires sliding on the snow-covered roads. "Careful there, Thunder boy. Take it easy now."

Collette's heart pounded as the truck driver managed to get back on his side of the road at the last second. She blew out her breath, pressing her hand to her chest. "*Ach,* that was close."

"And unexpected," said Colin, who looked as startled as she felt.

"That's one way to describe it," she agreed. "I hope he stays more in control before he hurts himself or someone else."

The next stop was Ben Gerstorf's home where they picked up a couple more games. Becky Gerstorf insisted they come in and have some pie, and they sat and chatted with the young couple until Colin announced they must get back on the road.

On their way again, Collette snuggled deeply under the buggy blanket and enjoyed the ride. The snow was still falling gently as they passed through the rolling countryside. Collette was filled with contentment; it was a lovely day, and she was thoroughly enjoying herself.

"Okay, next stop is the Frazier house," Colin announced as he snapped the reins. "We can head back after that and stop by the Kreigs' place on the way home."

"*Denki* for driving today, Colin," Collette told him. "I've enjoyed riding. It's been like a vacation day."

"I've enjoyed your company," he said. "I like talking with you."

"*Denki*," she answered, a blush creeping up her cheeks. She liked talking to him, too. He was intelligent and thoughtful and had a good sense of humor, too. "What do you think our next topic of conversation should be?"

"How about your *dat's* store? How are things going during these winter months?"

"Right fine. I like working there. I get to meet all kinds of people, locals and tourists alike. It's funny, don't you think, that we have tourists even when the weather is so cold?"

"Where are the tourists from who come the farthest?" he asked.

"I met a couple from Australia last week. They had wonderful accents. Although, I have to admit, they were a bit hard to understand."

"I'd love to see Australia someday," Colin said with a faraway look in his eyes. "With all its kangaroos and koalas."

"That would be exciting," she said. "Just think, you would have to fly over an ocean to get there."

"*Jah*. Imagine what it must look like from up there." Colin raised a finger skyward. "You must feel really close to *Gott*."

"*Jah*, with a bird's eye view."

They both laughed and continued chatting as they drove to the Frazier home. Michael and Debbie Frazier had half a dozen children all under the age of nine. Their stop there was filled with laughter and admiring children's drawings. Collette was still grinning when they left the home.

The rest of the ride back to her house seemed to go by quickly, and Collette felt a tinge of regret when it was over. She'd enjoyed spending the afternoon with Colin. He was easy going and liked to laugh. She was embarrassed to admit to herself that a part of her wished Ivan was more like Colin.

She stepped out of the buggy without really looking where she was stepping. Her foot landed on a patch of ice. Next thing she knew, she was flying through the air and landing hard on the ground.

The breath whooshed out of her, and she sat in shock with her mouth hanging open. Not only did her behind throb, but pain seared through her ankle.

"Collette, are you all right?" Colin cried after he rushed out of the buggy and around to her. He kneeled on the ground beside her, a worried look on his face.

"I-I think so... Could you help me up?" Collette swallowed down her pain as Colin helped her to her feet. But the moment she put weight on her ankle, she couldn't stop a little yip from escaping. She grasped Colin's arm to keep from falling.

"*Nee*, you are not okay," he said grimly, putting his arm more securely around her shoulders.

"*Ach*, I'll be all right." But she didn't feel all right. Her ankle throbbed with pain. Even so, she was acutely aware of Colin's arm and his proximity. Her face turned hot, and she knew she must be flushing bright red.

"I'm going to help you into the house. You'll need to get ice on that ankle right away." Colin spoke with calm authority, and she leaned into him.

"*Denki* for helping me," she said. Sudden guilt rushed through her. She was appreciating Colin way too much. She had a beau—what was she doing? She struggled a bit to free herself from Colin's arm, but he held on tightly.

They made it up the steps and across the porch to the front door. Collette reached down and grabbed the door handle and turned it, pushing the door wide open. She was tucked securely under Colin's arm when she looked up to see Ivan Yordy standing in front of her.

Chapter Ten

"What is going on here?" Ivan asked coldly as he stared at Collette cradled in Colin's arms. "Let her go, Fischer."

"I would, but she's hurt her ankle. She can't stand on it alone."

Mamm hurried forward and started questioning what happened, and *Daed* cleared a chair and motioned for Colin to bring her over and sit her down.

"I-I'm okay, I slipped on some ice and sprained my ankle, that's all." Collette could still feel the heat on her face.

"Let me get a pan of ice water," *Mamm* said and hurried off to the kitchen.

"We've got this now, Fischer. *Denki* for helping her in," Ivan said, standing with his hands on his hips.

"Of course. Take care of that ankle, Collette. I'll see you soon. *Gut* evening." Colin tipped his hat and left, and Collette suddenly felt a strange sense of loss creep through her.

"That was ... unexpected," Ivan said evenly.

"I didn't expect to fall," she shot back, irritated with his prim tone of voice. But as soon as the words left her mouth, she regretted them. What was wrong with her, anyway?

Daed raised an eyebrow and cleared his throat. "I'll help your mother with that ice water," he said, leaving the room.

"Collette, what's going on? You shouldn't have let him hold onto you like that."

"Hold onto me? *Ach*, Colin. He was helping me walk. What was I supposed to do? Crawl into the house?" Her temper, which rarely saw the light of day, was flaring now.

"You should have told Colin to come to the door and get your father or me," Ivan spoke stiffly. "That would have been much more seemly. Maybe you've been seeing too much of Colin Fischer, Collette. I don't want you to see him anymore, especially alone like you were today."

Collette's mouth dropped open in protest. Did he really just say that?

"I didn't even know you were here, so why would I even think to have you help me inside? And Colin is over at Esther's and Jesse's all the time. Of course, I'll see him. And if you had been more available lately and helping with the game night, I wouldn't have been alone with him."

Ivan pulled himself up straight, a hurt expression on his face. He seemed to be debating something internally for a moment before he said, "Collette, you're in pain right now so I'm going to forgive your harsh tone. I hope your ankle feels better soon. I think I'll be going now. I'll see you in a day or two, and we'll talk then."

Collette watched him put on his coat and walk out the door without saying a word.

He was going to forgive *her?* For her harsh tone? Well, that was certainly generous, wasn't it? A searing pain shot through her ankle, and she clenched her teeth against it. Goodness, but how quickly a lovely day could turn sour.

Even though she was feeling affronted, a wave of guilt washed over her. Truly, it must have been quite a shock for Ivan to see her basically in Colin Fischer's arms. She could only imagine what he must have thought when he saw them. Here she was suspicious of him because of a rumor, and he had actually *seen* her in another man's arms.

She didn't want to dwell on the thought of being cradled beneath Colin's muscular arm, but the burning of her skin where their bodies had come in contact wouldn't allow her to forget. There had been layers of clothing between her and Colin, but every nerve still tingled where they had connected.

Why did Colin have such an effect on her? No man should be able to make her skin tingle beside Ivan. She had been committed to Ivan for so long.

She needed to banish Colin from her thoughts. She closed her eyes and prayed. She knew she would need God's help to accomplish forgetting.

Colin guided Thunder into the barn and then got out to unhitch the horse. His mind wasn't on the job he was doing, though. He kept thinking about what it had felt like to hold Collette in his arms.

She was so tiny. She hardly weighed more than a bundle of shingles, and he hauled those two bundles at a time.

He'd hated to see the pain on her pretty face. He could see it cloud her clear eyes, lines of tension painting her forehead.

He had gathered her up instinctively to help her walk, but the moment he snuggled her under his arm a series of sensations washed over him. She smelled wonderful, like vanilla and honey. He had to fight the urge to hug her close, dip his head, and capture her lips beneath his own.

It seemed like bolts of lightning shot through his system making every nerve ending tingle and stand at alert. Her hands clutching him had felt hot even through her mittens.

The sensations were so strong, he was overwhelmed.

When the front door had swung open and revealed Ivan Yordy standing there like an angry judge, his stomach had taken a plunge. Ivan's stare raked over him like he was a plundering marauder stealing Ivan's woman. Her mother and father were there, too, both of them looking at him with their mouths open, their eyes full of concern for their daughter.

As he'd met Ivan's scathing gaze, he'd felt a spark of anger flare to life. This was the man who should have been with Collette this afternoon, but once again, he'd been absent. It was rumored that he was spending his time courting another woman. Was that where he'd been? Had he come to Collette's house after visiting another woman?

If so, Colin had no reason to feel guilty about being with Collette. Besides, he and Collette weren't courting—they were merely taking care of an errand for the youth Valentine's Day activity.

He did feel guilty about something else, though. He'd wanted to punch Ivan right in his smug face, and that was a sin. He'd have to ask God to forgive him, *again*... Not only for the urge to hit Ivan, but for thinking how satisfying it would be to ram his fist into Ivan's nose.

There was something else he needed to ask God for—he needed help in getting this desire for Collette out of his system. It was never going to work out. He couldn't indulge in daydreams of winning her away from Ivan. That wasn't how things were done. And it would only cause him pain in the long run. He would need God's help in shutting her out of his mind and out of his heart.

Colin led Thunder into his stall and leaned his head onto the horse's flank and closed his eyes, his hands grasping the silky strands of the horse's mane. He prayed for forgiveness for his anger at Ivan...and prayed even harder for help in squelching his feelings for Collette.

Chapter Eleven

Collette's ankle felt better after a couple of days' rest, and she could get around with just a slight limp. She spent her time mending and also working on the card she was making for Ivan for Valentine's Day.

She tried time and again to write a poem for the card, but nothing seemed quite right. She scratched out yet another line and chewed on the eraser end of the pencil, feeling frustrated. She was usually good with words and had a natural aptitude for poetry, but now when it was so important for her to express her feelings, the flow of words wasn't coming.

Ivan had not yet formally proposed to her, but she hoped he would ask her to marry him on Valentine's Day. She'd waited so long for him to declare himself. And Valentine's Day would be so romantic. It would be perfect.

She pictured Ivan's earnest expression, looking at her with love and yearning in his eyes. He would hold her hand and pledge his eternal love for her, promising to protect her and care for her the rest of his life.

Then something strange happened in her mind. Ivan's face morphed into the face of Colin Fischer, the blonde hair transforming into sable curls. Ivan's whip-cord thin body changed into broad shoulders and a muscular physique and Ivan's blue eyes altered into brown.

Collette blanched, taken aback by the sudden change in her mental painting of the scene. Why would Colin Fischer be on her mind now when she was dreaming of her future husband? Ivan was her one true love, wasn't he?

Dear Lord, what was happening to her?

She'd never thought about another man the way she thought of Ivan. Ivan had always been her hero, her bright and shining star. She couldn't possibly just replace him with another man, not even in her imagination.

Especially not Colin Fischer.

She shook the image away and went back to work on the card. Colin lingered in the background, despite her efforts to will him away. Yet somehow now, the words seemed to flow, and it wasn't long before she finished the card. She glued a tiny bow at the top and held it out and studied it. It was nice, truly nice.

She wouldn't even consider—especially to herself — that it might have been inspired by Colin Fischer, and not Ivan Yordy.

Colin strode the aisles of the hardware store on a mission to buy paint for the old Victorian home just a few blocks away, where he and his crew were working. They were redoing the hardwood floors and remodeling

63

the kitchen. It was going to be beautiful when it was finished.

The homeowners had already selected the color they wanted, so all he had to do was get it mixed and get the paint back to the job site. He waited his turn for help, looking around the store as he did. He glanced out the window, then did a double-take.

Was that Ivan Yordy standing on the sidewalk with a young blonde woman gazing up at him? Her hand rested on Ivan's arm and her chin was tilted up to look into his face. Any person could see she was in love with him.

A flare of burning anger sparked deep within Colin as he watched Ivan listen closely to something the blonde girl was saying. He nodded his head in agreement with her and smiled warmly. They turned as one and disappeared into Mary's Café.

Colin was still standing there fuming at the thought of Ivan being right there in public with this woman. He didn't doubt that this was the niece Esther had heard about. This woman and Ivan obviously knew each other well.

It came to his turn to order the paint, and he told the man he wanted three gallons. He glanced back out and saw Ivan reappear on the sidewalk and head toward the bank.

"I'll come back to pick that up in just a few minutes," he informed the man behind the counter. He turned and headed quickly out of the store. He strode purposefully toward the bank and waited outside until Ivan came back out.

"Ivan, I'd like a word with you," he called.

"Oh ... hello Colin, what can I do for you?"

"You can tell me why you're with that woman whose waiting for you in the café. I reckon she's the niece Esther Stutzman heard about, the one you're courting." Colin didn't mince words and didn't break eye contact with Ivan.

Ivan's gaze skittered away from Colin's, and Colin knew at once he was right. There had indeed been another woman Ivan was courting. Why had he dared bring her here to Baker's Corner where everyone could see them? Didn't he know he would be seen?

"What were you thinking, Yordy? Why did you bring her here where you were bound to be found out? How could you do this to Collette?" Colin's voice was cold and hard as he stared down the other man.

"Look, Colin, I didn't bring her here. She came with her mother to celebrate her *aenti's* birthday and looked me up. I couldn't avoid it."

"You couldn't avoid it? How about avoiding seeing two women at once? All I care about is you are going to hurt Collette. She needs to know what you've been up to. Are you going to tell her or am I?" Colin was grateful for his control. His prayers had been heard.

"Don't be like that. Please don't tell her." Ivan's blue eyes pleaded with Colin. "Nothing is going on between me and Iris. You just *thought* you saw something there."

"My eyes saw clearly what was going on. That girl looked at you like you hung the moon and stars. You are not being fair to her or Collette." He shook his head with disgust. "All your recent trips to Yellow Creek had nothing to do with helping your cousin, did they? It was always to see this Iris woman. Come on, Yordy. You'll tell Collette you've been seeing someone and right away. Or I will."

"Why don't you mind your own business?" Ivan growled. "Let me handle this my own way."

"You've got until this weekend to tell her or I will," Colin repeated his promise without flinching.

Ivan pursed his lips and tilted his chin then spun on his heel and stalked back to the café.

Colin stood in the middle of the sidewalk with his hands planted on his hips. By this weekend Ivan would tell her, or he would. Collette had to know. Dear Lord, he didn't want to be the one to tell her, but he would. *Ach,* Collette... This was going to break her heart.

He hoped Ivan Yordy would face responsibility and tell her himself. But he wasn't overly hopeful.

Chapter Twelve

Collette wiped the counter down and stood back and studied her surroundings. Everything was clean and spotless again. She had just finished baking dozens of cookies for the store, and her ankle reminded her she needed to get off her feet for a while.

"I think the baking's done for the day," she told Faith, another woman who worked in the kitchen. "And the kitchen is *redded* up to go again."

"*Jah*. We made *gut* time today. Now you need to sit down and rest. You're starting to limp a little more." Faith pulled a stool up to the counter. "Here, sit a spell."

"*Denki*, Faith. My ankle is a lot better, but it does still ache when I'm on it too long."

"Well, sit down and take a break. It's almost lunchtime, anyway." Faith opened the fridge and took out two cans of soda and gave one to Collette. "Here you are."

"*Denki*. A break does sound good. After lunch, we'll mix up more ham salad. Then our shift is over."

Collette leaned her head back and closed her eyes for a minute. She was tired, but it was a good fatigue achieved from hard work. She'd catch a second wind in a minute and get up and make a sandwich for lunch.

"Hi, Collette. Got a minute?"

Collette's eyes flashed with surprise when she turned and saw Esther standing behind her.

"Hi, Esther. What's up?"

Esther squirmed nervously as she chewed her bottom lip, then she sucked in a deep breath.

"I've got something to tell you, and you're not going to like it," she finally blurted out.

"What is it?" Collette snapped to attention, fear wriggling through her. It was something bad. "Come on, don't make me guess."

Esther paused until Faith took the hint and slipped away, leaving them alone.

"Ivan's at the café, and I'm pretty sure he's with that girl. The one I told you about before. I, well, I was walking past the café and looked in and there they were, at a booth by the window. I know she's not from around here, at least I've never seen her before, and they looked very...intent on one another."

"Are you serious?" Collette asked, getting to her feet and ignoring the throb in her ankle. "He's there now?"

"They were there a few minutes ago. When I didn't recognize her, I figured she must be from out of town. I came straight here after I saw them."

Collette stood for a moment, thoughts racing through her head. Just because he was with a girl didn't mean he was courting her, did it? Maybe she was a cousin or some other kin. It wouldn't do to assume the worst...

"I'm going down there," she said, making a snap decision. If she found the two of them together, he would have to introduce the girl, right? That would only be common courtesy, and her curiosity would be satisfied at the same time. It was a simple solution. "Are you coming with me?"

"*Jah*, I'll go," Esther agreed. "We'll take my buggy."

"I'll be back, Faith," Collette said as she pulled on her coat. "This shouldn't take long."

She'd go down there and find out there was a simple explanation. In fact, she'd be glad to put this whole rumor situation to rest. Ivan would tell her this girl was his cousin, and the suspicions would be gone.

A few minutes later, Esther tied up the horse a couple of doors down from the café, and the two women climbed out.

"We'll go in and I'll get a bite for lunch. If they're still there, we'll go over and talk to them, okay?"

"All right," Esther agreed, but her face was creased with concern.

Together they walked into the café, and Collette immediately saw Ivan seated at a booth with a young blonde woman across from him. She was talking animatedly and looking at him with adoring eyes.

Collette knew the minute she saw the look on the woman's face, that this was not a cousin. Her feet froze in their tracks, and she thought she could hear her heart crack.

"Ivan," she breathed.

Apparently, she had spoken his name louder than she'd thought because Ivan turned to face her. The color leeched out of his face, and he scrambled to his feet.

"Collette," he said, "I can explain."

She blinked and opened her mouth to speak, but nothing came out.

"This is Iris, Iris Shelter. She's from Yellow Creek." He spoke the introduction so quickly, Collette could hardly understand him. "She came with her mother to visit her *aenti*."

The smile fell from Iris's face as she looked in confusion from Collette to Ivan and then back to Collette.

Collette stared at the girl, suddenly understanding that Iris hadn't a clue she even existed. Iris had been deceived just like she had been.

Ivan had the grace to look shamefaced for a moment. That was all the confession Colette needed.

"Ivan, who is this?" Iris interrupted. "I don't understand what's going on."

"What's going on is he has been courting both of us," Collette told her, her voice returning with force. "We've both been played for fools."

"*Nee*, that's not how it is," Ivan objected.

"Isn't it, Ivan?" Collette asked, her voice acid.

Iris gasped and angry color flooded her cheeks.

"Is that why you've been acting so funny all day?" Iris demanded, her voice rising. "You didn't look happy when I surprised you this morning, and you didn't want to come out for lunch. Were you trying to hide me from your girlfriend? Is that it?"

Iris stood and choked on a sob. She looked at Collette. "I-I'm so sorry. I didn't know." She then stared at Ivan. "*Gut*-bye, Ivan. Don't bother to contact me again."

Collette watched her spin on her heel and run out of the café. Her own heart like lead, Collette glared at Ivan. She wasn't going to cry, not in front of him. "The same goes for me, Ivan. We're through."

It took strength for her to walk out of there with her head held high and her back straight. Esther quickly followed, and they hurried back to the buggy.

"Take me back to the store, please," Collette said, her voice tense.

"Collette," Esther questioned worriedly, "I'm so sorry. Are you okay?"

"I will be," Collette answered numbly. "I just want to go back to the store and make ham salad and not think about anything right now."

Esther remained silent and drove the buggy back to the store. Before Colette got out of the buggy, Esther turned her worried gaze on her cousin. She reached out and gave Collette a warm hug.

"I'm so, so sorry. *Gott* bless you, Collette. Things will work out. I know they will."

Collette couldn't speak, she just nodded and climbed out of the buggy. Pain pounded through her head and her heart. A giant fist squeezed her lungs. She fought to draw in a deep breath.

She paused at the back door and leaned against the wall. Cutting through the shocked pain was anger—anger and disgust.

How could Ivan court another woman at the same time he courted her? And after they had been seeing each other for years? How deceitful was that? And he had denied it. *Denied* it right to her face.

She thought she knew Ivan so well, and now...now it turned out he was a complete stranger.

Chapter Thirteen

Collette sat at Esther's table, amidst Esther, Jesse and Colin, her chin propped in her hands. She was spending the night with her cousin again. She didn't want to be alone with her thoughts.

She was still angry and somewhat disoriented, but now she was angrier at herself than at Ivan. She had been a blind fool. All the signs were right in front of her, and she had stubbornly ignored them like a naïve child.

"Don't be so hard on yourself, Collette," Esther said gently. "You've never dealt with a cheater before."

Collette snorted. "*Nee*, I haven't. I believed him, Esther. Even when he was lying right to me."

"Why wouldn't you? You trusted Ivan, you defended him when I suggested he might be stepping out on you. You were loyal and faithful."

"He might as well have slapped me in the face," Collette whispered, her eyes stinging with unshed tears.

Jesse and Colin sat in silent sympathy. They were all indulging in big slabs of chocolate sheet cake, but Collette's lay mainly untouched. She fiddled her fork around in some crumbs and continued to mentally berate herself.

How could she have been so blind? She thought she was smarter than that.

She remembered Ivan telling her she had his heart just a few weeks ago. He had sounded so sincere. He had denied seeing anyone else. If she couldn't trust him to tell the truth about that, how could she entrust her life and that of their future children to him?

Well, she wouldn't have to, now, would she? It was over.

A part of her was sending a strange message to her brain—what was it? *Relief?*

Surely not.

Yet she couldn't deny the small voice in her head that was celebrating. She had been under Ivan Yordy's spell since she was twelve years old. Enchanted by him, mesmerized by his charisma and good looks, captivated by the fact that he'd risked his life to save hers. It was as if she were suddenly freed from blindness.

"I don't understand," she said quietly, "why a part of me feels relieved this has happened."

"Because you trust that *Gott* has got this. He's got you," Colin said. "This happened for a reason. He has another plan for you. Your heart is trying to tell you that."

She nodded, soothed by his words of faith.

"You'll feel even better if you forgive Ivan, you know. When you're able." Colin's voice was soft and for a moment, there was something in his eyes—almost as if he were saying the words to himself, too. Had this upset him? It appeared so.

Collette let her gaze meet his. He looked back at her, his eyes filled with compassion. They studied each other for a long moment, and Collette felt something break loose in her heart. She would forgive Ivan for his lies and deception; she would.

But she would never trust him with her heart again. She had meant what she'd said. They were through.

As she gazed at Colin, she felt a bond stretch between them. She knew he felt her pain almost as deeply as she did, and he was offering her his strength to lean on.

"*Denki*, Colin," she murmured softly. "Those are wise words. I'll remember them."

She was still unable to turn away from his eyes. It was like a current connected them and at first, she couldn't move.

Finally, she shook her head and was able to force herself to look away. She suddenly remembered the Valentine's card she had made for Ivan, and in that moment, she knew it was Colin who had inspired it.

Confusion tumbled through her, and her head ached.

"I'm sorry. It's been a long day. I'm going to bed." She stood up and hurried to leave the room, their calls of good night following her.

Collette was upstairs putting her freshly laundered clothes away when she heard a buggy roll up the drive. She peeked out the window and recognized Ivan at the reins.

75

Ivan was here? Why? She had nothing more to say to him. Her stomach clenched as she watched him climb out of the buggy and stride to the door. She recognized that gait—he walked in such a way when he was intent on something. Was he planning to confront her?

She groaned. She wasn't used to confrontation, but she was determined to stand her ground. She wanted nothing more to do with Ivan Yordy.

"Collette, Ivan is here. Do you want to see him?" her mother called up the stairway.

"I'd rather not," she said as she peered down the stairs.

"Please, Collette, let me talk to you." Ivan stepped forward to the base of the steps, his hat in his hands.

"There's nothing to talk about, Ivan. I told you, we're through."

"*Ach,* don't say that. You don't mean it." He glanced at her mother as she slipped out of the room and left them. "At least, come down for a minute."

If that was what it took to get rid of him, she would comply. She grasped the handrail and descended the stairs to where he stood.

"I mean it, Ivan. There is nothing left between us. Your deceit killed anything we had."

He looked shamefaced, but it didn't stop him from pleading his case. "I was a fool. I felt like I was in a ... a trap or something. I wanted to explore a bit. We'd been together so long, and I hadn't ever tried courting anyone else. I gave in to temptation."

She looked at him sadly. "I was a ... *trap? Ach*, Ivan. That is horrid." She inhaled deeply. "Well, you made your choice. You chose to lie to me and to deceive me. I will forgive you, but I won't subject myself to you again. You should be happy. You're no longer *trapped*. Now, I think you should leave."

She was trembling, but she didn't waver, and she kept her gaze on him steadfast.

"But, Collette, I..." he sputtered.

"*Nee*. There's nothing more between us. We'll treat each other politely in the future, but that's all."

He looked at her, and it was clear he finally believed her. His voice was shaky as he said, "You really mean it, don't you?"

"I do. I want to get on with my life, and you have no place in it."

Slow red climbed up his cheeks, and he stared at her a moment longer. Then he jutted out his jaw and walked out.

She watched him go and gave thanks to God for sparing her a lifetime with this man.

"You know, Jesse, if I were Catholic instead of Amish, I'd probably be setting in a confessional right now," Colin spoke while he forked hay into the stall for Thunder.

"That's an odd thing to say. Have you committed some great sin I'm not aware of?"

"*Nee*, but I can't help feeling *gut* about Ivan and Collette splitting up. I know I shouldn't, that it has caused her pain, but she'll be better off in the end. Ivan wasn't *gut* enough for her."

"I think you're feeling guilty because you hope you can take advantage of the situation. You're smitten with her, *ain't so?*"

Colin paused and leaned on the pitchfork. Jesse was right. He was smitten with Collette. More than smitten, truth be told. He thought about her all the time. She was the last thing he thought of at night and the first thing on his mind in the morning. Goodness, he even dreamed about her a lot of nights.

In his dreams, they were married and surrounded by children. They lived there in the house he had purchased the year before, and they were all well and happy. He watched as his dream family ate and played together. He watched as their children were tucked into bed and kissed good night.

Then it was his turn to kiss Collette good night.

"Hey, Colin, come back to earth. You look about a thousand miles away." Jesse grinned at him and slapped him on the back. "Are you dreaming about my little cousin?"

Colin's face heated in embarrassment. "Sorry. I can't help but want to rush in and offer to take Ivan's place. I know I can't do that, though. She just got out of a relationship. I doubt if she wants to rush right into another one."

"You never know, Colin. Maybe she'll see the light sooner rather than later."

"I'll just be happy if I can eventually make her mine. I'm going to have to be patient."

"Well, I wish you *Gott's* blessings, my friend. I think you and Collette are well-suited."

"*Denki*, Jesse. I'm going to ask *Gott* for patience and wait and see what happens."

Chapter Fourteen

This time Esther was staying at Colette's house for the night. They were dressed for bed and sitting cross-legged on the twin beds in Collette's room.

"You seem like you're feeling better today, Collette," Esther said as she ran a brush through her own waist-length hair.

"I am. It all seems so odd now. Almost like it happened to someone else. *Ach,* Esther, I might have made the biggest mistake of my life." She toyed with the fabric of her long flannel nightgown. "And I might have missed out on a big blessing I think might come."

"What's that mean?" Esther paused, tilting her head inquisitively.

Collette was silent for a moment. She debated how much to say to her cousin. She'd only recently allowed herself to ponder on it much. But Esther was not only her cousin; she was her best friend. She drew in a breath and then said, "I know you might think me crazy but I ... I like Colin. It's fast, I know. Up until a few of days ago, I thought I would be marrying Ivan. Now I've done a complete turnaround. I don't know... Maybe I felt like I owed Ivan something for saving my life all those years ago. Maybe I thought it was meant to be. Anyway, whatever it was, it blinded me to a ... a wonderful *gut* man standing right in front of me."

Esther's brow rose to the top of her forehead and then she smiled. "Seriously, Collette? Do you think you might actually love Colin?"

Collette knew the answer. She *did* love Colin. She simply hadn't seen it.

She knew how she felt when their eyes met. It was like drowning in pools of warmth and kindness. She recalled how easily they'd laughed and talked on the buggy ride to collect the games, how natural being with him felt.

A smile tugged at the corner of her lips. "I believe I do. But I ... need to think on it more. And I have no idea if he returns my feelings at all." But she prayed he did. How she prayed he did.

"I think you should tell him how you feel. Be honest with him."

"*Nee,* Esther, I couldn't. It would be so forward. And I only just got out of one relationship. *Nee,* I can't tell him."

"Well, it's your decision, but I think you need to take a chance. I've got a feeling you might be surprised." Esther paused and looked at her. "I've seen the way he looks at you, Collette. I've got a strong feeling he feels the same way you do."

Collette let her cousin's words wash over her. If only that were true... Was it possible? Should she open up to Colin and risk her heart again?

~

Valentine's Day was on Sunday, so they were holding their game activity the day before. Collette spent the morning baking brownies and making a big batch of chili to serve after they finished ice skating. The other women would bring food, too, so there would be a good selection to choose from.

Collette had planned on going to this event with Ivan, but that, of course, was now out of the question. *Daed* was driving her to Esther's, and she would ride the rest of the way with Esther and Jesse.

"Hi, Collette," Jesse greeted her later that day, taking the pot of chili from her after *Daed* pulled up in front of their house. "I hope you're ready to have some fun tonight."

"More than ready. Is Esther ready to go?"

"Just about. Go on in, and I'll put this pan in the buggy."

Esther was just pulling on her coat when Collette walked in

"Hello. Grab that pan of popcorn balls, will you, and I'll take the cake I made."

"Okay. Have you got your skates?"

"They're already in the buggy. I see you've got yours," she nodded at the skates Collette had tied together and hung over her shoulder.

"*Jah*, I'm ready to skate. I've got my long underwear on under my stockings, so I won't freeze."

"Me, too." Esther laughed. "Let's go then."

The girls headed out and climbed into the buggy, drawing the lap robe across them. Soon the horse was trotting down the road on the way to the Kraus's home, pulling into the drive twenty-five minutes later.

They went into the house and put down their contributions to the party, then headed out to the pond down the hill. The men had built a fire near the edge of the water, and it was the perfect setting for a skating party.

Collette sat on a bench and put on her skates. She looked around and tried to spot Colin, but she didn't see him anywhere. He must not have arrived yet.

She and Esther made their way onto the ice and after a few wobbly starts, Collette let herself relax and enjoy the activity. She loved to skate, loved the feeling of gliding along so smoothly. She laughed out loud as the snow began to fall and a flake landed on her nose.

She looked out across the ice and nearly stumbled. Ivan was there, and he'd brought Iris Shelter with him. Collette did a double-take, not believing her eyes. But it was true. Evidently, Iris hadn't given Ivan up, after all. She took in a slow breath. What nerve Ivan had, bringing her here so soon after their break-up.

At that moment, Esther slid to a stop beside her.

"He's here," she said, under her breath. "And with that girl."

"I know," Collette answered evenly. She waited for the pain that was sure to accompany such a sight. She waited for her heart to twist inside her. But it didn't come.

It *didn't come*.

She blinked rapidly, searching herself for sorrow or hurt or anger. And then she nearly laughed. Nothing. She felt nothing. Was that normal? She shook her head and did laugh now.

Esther was gaping at her. "What's so funny? Are you laughing?"

"Esther, I don't feel bad. I don't even care. Ivan and Iris can skate right beside me if they want to. I don't care."

Never had Collette felt such freedom. She could look at Ivan now and not see a hero. She only saw a regular man with his share of flaws.

The revelation made her feel light and happy.

With another laugh, Collette took off around the pond again, Esther by her side. After what must have been a full hour, all the skaters grew weary and decided it was time to go to the house. It was getting dark, and everyone was becoming hungry.

Colin still hadn't shown up, and Collette was starting to worry. She sat at a card table next to Esther and asked her if she'd heard anything from him.

"*Nee,* I haven't. I was sure he'd be here by now, even if he didn't want to skate. I know he'll want to eat," she said with a grin. "Colin does love to eat."

"And yet he's not here," Collette fretted. "I think something might be wrong."

She had a flashback to the night Ivan had gone missing when he was supposed to come to pick her up. He'd been up to no good... But this wasn't that, she told herself, not in this case. Besides, she and Colin had no understanding. This was completely different. Still, Colin had worked hard with her

84

organizing the games. It wasn't like him to ignore all the plans they had made. She knew he wouldn't.

It was only a few minutes later when Jesse appeared at their table.

"Hey, we just got word. Colin was riding his bicycle over here and hit a patch of ice and tumbled down a hill. I guess he's pretty banged up."

Collette's stomach plunged. He was hurt? Dear *Gott*, don't let his injuries be too serious.

"I'm going now to go check on him," Jesse said.

"I'm coming with you," Collette declared and shot Jesse a do-not-argue-with-me glare.

"Well, get your coat, and let's go then." He didn't argue with her. He clearly knew that look.

Collette sat on the edge of her seat as the buggy rolled toward Colin's house. He couldn't be hurt too badly, she assured herself. If so, he'd be at the hospital, not at home.

But she was still worried. She wouldn't be satisfied until she saw for herself that he was all right. When they pulled in his drive, she jumped out of the buggy and ran toward the porch with Jesse right behind her.

Jesse went right on in, and Collette's heart clenched when she saw Colin's battered face. He had a black eye and a big scratch running down his cheek. One of his legs was propped up on a pillow.

"*Ach,* Colin, I'm so sorry you're hurt," she cried when she saw him. "But thank *Gott* you're in one piece."

Colin smiled, then grimaced. "I should have been paying more attention. I didn't even see the patch of ice I hit. Before I knew it, I had hit the ice and went flying head over heels before I could do anything about it. Marvin Stoltzfus helped me back home. Was he the one that told you I got banged up?"

"He's the one. That's a great shiner, Colin," Jesse teased. "I'd hate to see the other guy."

"She doesn't have a scratch on her," Colin confessed drolly. "I clearly lost this round with Mother Nature."

"Well, better luck next time. But seriously, is there anything you need? Whatever it is, I'll take care of it for you."

"I'm *gut. Denki,* Jesse. I'm just going to eat a bit of soup and go to bed."

Collette watched him carefully. He seemed to be okay. She could breathe easier now as far as his welfare was concerned. But now she had a new worry.

She knew for sure the feelings she had for Colin Fischer were far more than friendship. The problem was, what did she do about that now?

Chapter Fifteen

Collette didn't sleep well that night. She couldn't stop thinking about Colin. What if he had been killed yesterday? She'd only just discovered her true feelings for him, and had then almost lost him without telling him how she felt.

She got up early and sat in the chair next to the window, looking out at the breaking dawn. It was a new day, and she needed a new plan for her life.

After breakfast, she decided to go get Esther and take her with her to call on Colin. She could hardly go to his house alone. But she needed to see him, and she wanted to deliver the Valentine's Day card she'd made for him. After all, it had been him she was thinking of when she wrote that poem. It was never meant for Ivan. She knew that now.

So, she had re-written the poem into a new card. This time, a card for Colin—as it should have been in the first place.

Collette brushed her hair and put on a fresh apron before she bundled up and went outside to hitch up the buggy. She put a thermos of soup and the new Valentine's Day card in the back of the buggy and drove straight to Esther's house. She figured they had time before the preaching service that morning.

"Come on. We're going to check on Colin and take him something to eat," she told Esther without any more explanation.

Her cousin looked at her curiously, but she didn't question her. She told her mother she'd be at service later and just got her coat and went out to the buggy with Collette. Within minutes, they were on their way to Colin's house.

Colin's eye was even more colorful this morning, and the scratch on his face was a vivid red. He moved stiffly but greeted them with a smile.

"We've come to make sure you get fed," Collette informed him. "I brought you a thermos of soup. But we can also make you some eggs if you like."

The two women moved efficiently around his small kitchen and along with the thermos of soup, soon produced a breakfast of pancakes, fried eggs, and hash brown potatoes. Colin moaned in anticipation as he took a seat, and Esther poured coffee into his cup.

Collette was prepared to hand him the card, she truly was, but she lost her nerve. Instead, she took it from its current hiding place beneath the folds of her apron and left it on a table by the front door when they were leaving.

Now the next move would be his. She whispered a prayer as she left the envelope on the table and slipped out the door.

Then she had to wait. She drove Esther to preaching service, where she thought the sermons would never end. At first, she was filled with anticipation regarding Colin's response to her card. Then she was filled with dread. What had she done? He would think she was way too forward and immodest—for the poem exposed her feelings completely.

She fretted as she helped set out the community meal. She worried as she helped clean up afterward. She was almost silent when she dropped Esther off and went on home.

That afternoon, she was so restless, she couldn't sit still.

Mamm set aside the book she was reading and eyed Collette with concern. "What's wrong, *dochder*? Are you worrying about Ivan again?"

Collette shook her head and chewed on her bottom lip before deciding to tell her mother what was really on her mind.

"Oh, *mamm*, I may have done something really foolish." She went on to explain how she felt about Colin. "I know it sounds silly because I thought I was in love with Ivan just a few days ago, and now I know I never truly loved him. I was grateful to him. I thought I owed him my life, but I was wrong. I-I left Colin a card telling him how I feel."

Dorothy wrapped her arm around Collette's shoulders. "So, now you know the difference between gratitude and love. *Ach*, daughter, don't fret. It will all work itself out."

"Do you really think so?" Collette asked, looking at her mother with tears in her eyes.

"I know so. Do you know how I know? You're listening to your heart." Collette shook her head but Dorothy went on. "And besides, I just saw Colin's buggy pull in the driveway."

Collette gasped and whirled to look out the window in time to see Colin climbing out of the buggy and limping toward the door. Her hands flew to her cheeks, and her heart hammered crazily in her chest.

Colin was *here*. That was a good thing, wasn't it? Dear *Gott*, let it be a good thing. Or maybe he was here to tell her she was way off base, that he felt nothing toward her.

She held her breath until his knock came at the door. Her mother's gaze met her wide eyes, and a smile quirked her lips as she went to open the door.

"*Gut* evening, Colin. Come in." She swung the door wide and stepped back. "I was just going to get something from my room, but Collette will be happy to help you with whatever you need, won't you, Collette?"

Her mother quickly disappeared up the stairs.

Collette had trouble making herself look into Colin's eyes, but she took a deep breath and raised her gaze to meet his. She didn't breathe until she saw the sweet smile spread across his face. He didn't have to say a word—his expression said it all.

Yet he did speak. "Happy Valentine's Day, Collette. I brought you something." He held out a bag of chocolate chips and laughed. "Sorry, I didn't have anything else. I-I wasn't prepared. But I am hoping you'll come to dinner with me soon. I think we have a lot to talk about."

Joy bubbled within her heart as she gazed into Colin's beautiful, bruised face.

"Do we, Colin? *Ach*, I hope so. I hope we have lots to talk about."

"Will tomorrow evening suit? I can pick you up around five-thirty. That should give us plenty of time." He grinned and took her hand. "Plenty of time to talk about our future."

Happiness washed over her, and she couldn't stop smiling. Her mother had been right.

Collette could hear exactly what her heart was saying now.

The End

Continue Reading...

Thank you for reading ***The Valentine's Day Card!*** Are you **wondering what to read next?** Why not read ***A Secret Fresh Start?* Here's a peek for you:**

Eleanor Chupp watched her mother tremulously draw her last breath and could actually feel Margaret Chupp's soul leave her body as the rising and falling of her chest slowed, then became still. It was almost as if her mother did not want to see another New Year begin, so she decided to simply go away. The time was just shy of midnight on New Year's Eve.

Eleanor felt a numbness wash over her. She couldn't conceive that her mother's battle was over. After struggling with cancer three times over the past six years, her mother was truly gone. The pain was over...her *mamm* was no more.

Eleanor drew her gaze from the fragile shell of a woman on the bed to look at her father. His stern face was set as if carved in stone, his eyes granite hard. For a moment Eleanor thought she saw his chin tremble, but he immediately squared his jaw and turned and left the room.

Eleanor would have loved to have thrown herself into *Daed's* arms and to cry her broken heart out...but *Daed* wasn't the kind of man who would allow it. He hated weakness. He did not show affection. He was gruff, unyielding, disciplined. He would not welcome a weeping daughter, no matter what the occasion.

For a moment or two, she couldn't move. She was frozen, feeling as if a part of her had died as well. She'd dedicated the last six years of her life to caring for her mother, helping her fight the battles, making her the most nutritious meals she knew how to create. She'd spent hours on her knees, praying that it was *Gott's* will that Margaret overcame this illness. Twice her mother had battled back against aggressive cancer, twice they thought she had won. Then came the third time.

Margaret was only forty years old. She had been young, strong and healthy, and was always happy and cheerful. Everyone thought she would be able to win the war against breast cancer. But in the end, it hadn't worked out that way; cancer had metastasized throughout her body.

Her father, Abraham, was older, sixty-two years old, and didn't seem to possess a sense of humor. He was a deacon in their church and well-respected in their community, but he had a reputation for inflexibility and rigidity. Eleanor thought her parents were a match of opposites.

She remembered her mother telling her once why she had married Abraham. Abraham was her second husband, after she'd been widowed just six months after her first marriage took place.

VISIT HERE To Read More!
https://www.ticahousepublishing.com/amish-miller.html

Thank you for Reading

More Amish Romance from Hannah Miller

Visit HERE for Hannah Miller's Amish Romance

https://ticahousepublishing.com/amish-miller.html

About the Author

Hannah Miller has been writing Amish Romance for the past seven years. Long intrigued by the Amish way of life, Hannah has traveled the United States, visiting different Amish communities. She treasures her Amish friends and enjoys visiting with them. Hannah makes her home in Indiana, along with her husband, Robert. Together, they have three children and seven grandchildren. Hannah loves to ride bikes in the sunshine. And if it's warm enough for a picnic, you'll find her under the nearest tree!

Made in United States
North Haven, CT
23 July 2025

70954220R00055